A NOTE TO PARENTS

Disney's **First Readers Level 1** books were developed with the beginning reader in mind. They feature large, easy-to-read type, lots of repetition, and simple vocabulary.

One of the most important ways parents can help their child develop a love of reading is by providing an *environment* of reading. Every time you discuss a book, read aloud to your child, or your child observes you reading, you promote the development of early reading skills and habits. Here are some tips to help you use **Disney's First Readers Level 1** books with your child:

★ Tell the story about the original Disney film or video. Storytelling is crucial to language development. A young child needs a language *foundation* before reading skills can begin to emerge.

★ Talk about the illustrations in the book. Beginning readers need to use illustrations to gather clues about unknown words or to understand the story.

★ Read aloud to your child. When you read aloud, smoothly run your finger under the text. Do not stop at each word. Enliven the text for your child by using a different voice for each character. In other words, be an actor—and have fun!

★ "Read it again!" Children love hearing stories read again and again. When they begin reading on their own, repetition helps them feel successful. Maintain patience, be encouraging, and expect to read the same books over and over.

★ Play "question and answer." Use the After-Reading Fun activities provided at the end of each book to further enhance your child's learning process.

Remember that early-reading experiences that you share with your child can help him or her to become a confident and successful reader later on!

— Patricia Koppman
Past President
International Reading Association

Pencils by Denise Shimabukuro

First published by Disney Press, New York, New York.
This edition published by Scholastic Inc.,
90 Old Sherman Turnpike, Danbury, Connecticut 06816
by arrangement with Disney Licensed Publishing.

SCHOLASTIC and associated logos are trademarks of Scholastic Inc.

ISBN 0-7172-6462-9

Printed in the U.S.A.

Where's Flit?

by Bettina Ling
Illustrated by Eric Binder and Darren Hont

Disney's First Readers — Level 1
A Story from Disney's *Pocahontas*

SCHOLASTIC INC.

New York   Toronto   London   Auckland   Sydney
Mexico City   New Delhi   Hong Kong   Buenos Aires

"Let's go see Grandmother Willow," Pocahontas calls to Flit and Meeko.

"There is the
path. Come on,
let's go."

As Meeko leads the way, Pocahontas stops to say, "Where's Flit?"

Here's a good place to hide.
Pocahontas looks inside.
No Flit.

Pocahontas looks in a tree.
What's up there?
Whose nest does she see?
Not Flit's.

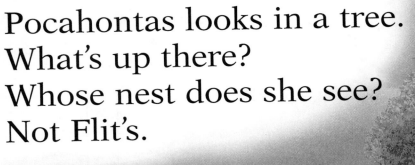

Meeko hears a sound.
He looks all around.
No Flit.

Is Flit down a hole?

Or inside the log?

Or in the mud
with one tiny frog?

Pocahontas reaches water.
She sees fish and
an otter.

But no Flit.

Where else can they look?
Where else can they go?

Maybe Grandmother Willow
will know.

Pocahontas leads the way.
She is just about to say,
"Where's Flit?"

Now, who do they see
in the old willow tree?

It's Flit!

AFTER-READING FUN

Enhance the reading experience with follow-up questions to help your child develop reading comprehension and increase his/her awareness of words.

Approach this with a sense of play. Make a game of having your child answer the questions. You do not need to ask all the questions at one time. Let these questions be fun discussions rather than a test. If your child doesn't have instant recall, encourage him/her to look back into the book to "research" the answers. You'll be modeling what good readers do and, at the same time, forging a sharing bond with your child.

Where's Flit?

1. **Where does this story take place?**

2. **Who does Pocahontas want to visit?**

3. **Is Flit really lost?**

4. **Name some places where Pocahontas looks for Flit.**

5. **Where is your favorite place to hide? Why?**

6. **How many two-letter words can you find in the story?**